THE HUNTER'S CODE

BY JAKE MADDOX

illustrated by Sean Tiffany

text by Bob Temple

Librarian Reviewer
Chris Kreie
Media Specialist, Eden Prairie Schools, MN
MS in Information Media, St. Cloud State University, MN

Reading Consultant
Mary Evenson
Middle School Teacher, Edina Public Schools, MN
MA in Education, University of Minnesota

STONE ARCH BOOKS
www.stonearchbooks.com

Impact Books are published by Stone Arch Books
151 Good Counsel Drive, P.O. Box 669
Mankato, Minnesota 56002
www.stonearchbooks.com

Library of Congress Cataloging-in-Publication Data
Maddox, Jake.
    The Hunter's Code / by Jake Maddox; illustrated by Sean Tiffany.
    p. cm. — (Impact books. A Jake Maddox Sports Story)
    ISBN 978-1-4342-0782-1 (library binding)
    ISBN 978-1-4342-0878-1 (pbk.)
    [1. Hunting—Fiction. 2. Responsibility—Fiction.] I. Tiffany, Sean,
ill. II. Title.
PZ7.M25643Hun 2009
[Fic]—dc22   2008004289

Summary: Ethan knows that killing animals for fun is against the
Hunter's Code. Or does he?

Art Director: Heather Kindseth
Graphic Designer: Kay Fraser

    Printed in the United States of America in Stevens Point, Wisconsin.
082009
0005601R

TABLE OF CONTENTS

CHAPTER 1
DAD IS HOME

Ethan heard the old truck coming down the street. The rumble of the truck was easy to hear. He knew exactly what that noise meant. His dad was home from his hunting trip.

Ethan's dad had spent the last five days in the north woods with his hunting buddies. His father took the same trip every year at the start of the deer hunting season.

For as long as Ethan could remember, he'd been hearing stories about his dad's hunting trips.

Dad had a nice car that he drove to work every day. But when it came time to head off on a hunting trip, he drove his old, beat-up pickup truck. It was the one that made lots of noise.

When Ethan heard the rumble of that truck on Sunday evening, he knew his father was almost home from the trip. There was just one thing to find out. Had Dad gotten a deer?

Ethan tried to act cool, but his eyes went straight to the window. His mom noticed his excitement. "Sounds like your dad's home," she said. "Why don't you go outside and meet him?"

Smiling, Ethan ran for the door. He pushed the screen door open just as the old truck pulled into the driveway. As the truck moved up closer to the house, Ethan stood on his tiptoes. He tried to see into the bed of the pickup.

Then he saw it. There it was, as plain as day. It was poking out above the edge of the truck — a buck's antlers.

CHAPTER 2
SEVEN-POINTER

As soon as the truck's engine died, Ethan ran to the driveway. He jumped over the side of the pickup and into the back. The face of a dead deer stared straight back at him.

"Awesome!" Ethan shouted.

He tried to guess how much the huge deer weighed. The number of points on the deer's antlers would tell him more about the deer. Ethan counted them quickly.

"Three, four, five, six!" he said. "A six-pointer! Nice job, Dad!"

Ethan's father slammed the truck door and walked toward the bed of the truck. "Uh, I think you missed one, buddy," he said, smiling.

Ethan looked again. There was another point! "Seven!" he shouted. "Nice!"

"So, what happened?" Ethan asked. "Which day did you get him? What time of day was it? Was this the only buck you guys got?"

"Slow down, buddy," his father said. "Let's go inside, and I'll tell you all about it after I get cleaned up."

"Good idea," Ethan replied. "You stink."

They both laughed. Then Ethan's dad headed inside the house.

While his dad took a shower, Ethan stayed in the back of the truck. He studied the deer, trying to learn as much as he could about the hunt on his own.

He carefully looked at the side of the animal, being careful not to touch the deer since it hadn't been cleaned. After a few seconds, Ethan found the place where the gunshot had entered the deer's body.

Just behind the front leg, a little ways up the side, he thought to himself. *That's a great shot.*

Every year when he got back from a trip, Ethan's dad had new stories. His father would repeat the funny stories he'd heard from his friends. He would talk about the cool things that had happened on the trip. Ethan loved the stories.

As he sat in the back of the truck, Ethan thought about the stories. When his dad told the stories, Ethan could almost see a buck come in close. He could imagine how it would feel to line up and take the shot.

Every year, Ethan's dad would say, "When you're old enough, you'll be coming along on these trips."

The words always sent a chill down Ethan's spine. He could feel the excitement building inside him. But it always sounded so far away. "When you're old enough." When would that be? When would he finally be old enough?

Every year, Ethan hoped it would finally be the year that he was old enough. He felt himself getting closer and closer. His dad had started to teach him stuff about hunting.

Ethan learned to hold a gun. He learned how to sight his target through the scope. He learned all the safety rules. But the most important thing his dad taught him was about the Hunter's Code.

"Never shoot anything just for the sport. You have to respect the animal," his father always said. "If you don't plan to eat it, you better not shoot it."

CHAPTER 3

Ten minutes later, Ethan's dad appeared in the doorway. "Come inside, Ethan," he called. "I want to tell you all about the trip."

Ethan ran inside. "So what happened?" he asked. "I want to hear everything."

His dad smiled. "It was great," he said. "Well, actually, it didn't start off great. For the first couple of days, none of the guys got anything."

"Oh, man!" Ethan said. "That must have been boring."

"Not really," Dad said. "We had a great time anyway."

"So when did you get the deer?" Ethan asked.

"Well, finally, we went out this morning for just a couple of hours," Dad said. "We were about to call it quits, but just as we were packing up, I heard something moving in the bushes."

Ethan leaned forward in his chair, listening carefully to every word.

His father went on, "Just then, out walked the buck. He was about 40 yards away from me. After a couple of minutes, I had a clear view. I took the shot. The single shot hit the deer and it fell."

"Sounds like a good shot, Dad," Ethan said.

"Yeah, it was, if I do say so myself," Dad said. "It was fast. That's a good thing, too," he added, "because you don't want the deer to feel pain."

"Right," Ethan said. "I know. That would be mean."

"That's right," Dad said. "You'll make a great hunter."

Ethan waited for the rest of the story — the line that he heard every year. He didn't move. He was waiting for his father to say, "When you are old enough."

But this time, the words were different.

"I got a little something for you when I was up there," Ethan's father said. "I hope you like it."

He reached behind the couch and pulled out a long, thin box.

Ethan grabbed it. He popped the box open and gasped. It was a brand-new, high-powered air gun.

CHAPTER 4
NOT A TOY

Ethan slowly pulled the air gun from the box. As he held it, he admired its long, lean shape. He felt the cool, smooth black metal and smiled widely.

"Unbelievable," he said. "This is awesome! Thanks, Dad!"

"I'm glad you like it," Dad said. "But before you can use it, you need to understand the power that it has."

"What do you mean?" Ethan asked. "It's not a real hunting gun. It can't be that dangerous."

"You're wrong about that," Dad replied, frowning. "It isn't powerful enough to use on a hunting trip. But it could really hurt someone. This gun packs a lot of power. The pellets that come out could seriously hurt someone. So you need to treat this gun like a real gun."

"Okay," Ethan said.

"This is not like the BB guns that you had as a kid," Dad said. "If you got hit with one of those, it wasn't a big deal. This type of gun could send a pellet through the skin. It could really hurt someone."

"Okay, I got it, Dad," Ethan said. "I promise I'll be careful."

"I signed you up for a firearm safety class," Dad said. "Once you get done with that, I'll teach you everything I know. This is going to be really fun. You just need to remember that this gun is not a toy."

Ethan nodded. "I'll remember. Don't worry, Dad," he promised.

CHAPTER 5
SAFE AIM

The firearm safety classes started after school the very next afternoon. Ethan was pretty excited to go to the first class. Along with a dozen other kids, Ethan got to learn how to safely aim and shoot a gun.

They learned a lot about hunting. They also learned a lot about taking care of guns, how to load a gun and clean it, and safety tips for being in the woods. Ethan thought it was a pretty fun class.

The class lasted for a few hours every day for a week. Finally, Ethan earned his Firearm Safety certificate.

After Ethan had earned his certificate, it was time to start learning from his dad.

Ethan's family lived a few miles out of town. Their backyard was a big forest. It was a great place to play. It was also a good place to practice shooting.

After school one day, Ethan and his dad headed out into the woods. It was getting dark, but there was still enough light coming through the treetops that they could see clearly.

Ethan's father brought along some old cans to use as targets. He carefully showed Ethan how to load the pellets into his gun. Then he showed him how to line up the target through the gun's scope.

Ethan peered through the scope. He aimed carefully at the root beer can that was his target. He pointed the gun at one of the Os in "root." Slowly, carefully, Ethan pulled the trigger.

Pffft! The gun fired. The gun's noise wasn't sharp and loud like the sound of a gunshot. Still, the power of the gun made Ethan jerk back.

Ethan lowered the gun and flicked the safety back on so that he wouldn't accidentally fire the gun again.

He looked at the root beer can, which was about 25 yards away.

The can was still standing up. It hadn't moved an inch.

Dad laughed. "Try it again, son," he said.

Ethan made another shot. But again, the can didn't move.

Dad frowned. "I wonder if there's something wrong with the sight on the gun," he said. "Can I take a look?"

Ethan handed him the gun. "Go ahead," Ethan said.

His father looked closely at the gun. "See, if it isn't set up right, you could be aiming at something that you're not looking at," he explained to Ethan. "That would cause a bad shot for sure."

Dad aimed the gun at the root beer can and pulled the trigger. *PFFT!* With a burst of noise, the can flew off the post it had been sitting on.

Ethan frowned. "I guess it works," he said quietly.

Dad looked at the gun and shook his head. "Well," he said, "everything seems to be set up right. Try it again."

Ethan fired the gun 20 or 30 more times that night. He never hit one of his targets. Not even once.

"It can be very difficult to hold steady at the target as you get ready to fire," Ethan's father said as they walked back toward the house. "Even the smallest movement can cause you to miss a small target like a can. Tomorrow night, we'll try something bigger. Don't worry, you'll get it."

Ethan nodded. But he wasn't sure he'd ever be able to hit his target. If he couldn't hit a dumb metal can, how could he ever hit a deer?

CHAPTER 6
TARGET PRACTICE

The next night, instead of using cans for target practice, Ethan's dad set up a huge piece of wood. He marked the middle with a bright green sticker.

Ethan aimed for the center, but his first shot barely hit the target. But he'd still hit it! He couldn't believe it.

"I hit it!" he yelled happily.

His dad smiled. "Good job," he said.

Ethan's next shot was closer to the center of the target, but it was still far from hitting it. But he didn't give up.

He just kept trying. And the more he shot, the closer he got to the center.

The next night, Dad cut the piece of plywood down to make it smaller. He made it even smaller the night after that. And soon, Ethan could hit a root beer can from 30 yards away.

By the time the next hunting season came, the combination of Ethan's gun safety class and his father's tutoring had made him better at using the gun. He felt really good about his skills.

One day in early November, Ethan was eating breakfast. His dad walked into the kitchen.

"You can shoot after school without me," he told Ethan, "as long as you shoot in the woods behind our house. And you have to make sure to follow all the safety rules. If you keep improving the way you have been, you may be ready for a real deer hunt this year."

Ethan was thrilled. He'd been waiting all his life for a real deer hunt. He knew what that meant. A real hunt, a real gun, a real target.

Finally, he'd be one of the guys. He'd be treated like a grownup. It would be amazing.

That afternoon after school, Ethan headed out in the woods behind the house. He made sure the area was safe. He loaded his gun.

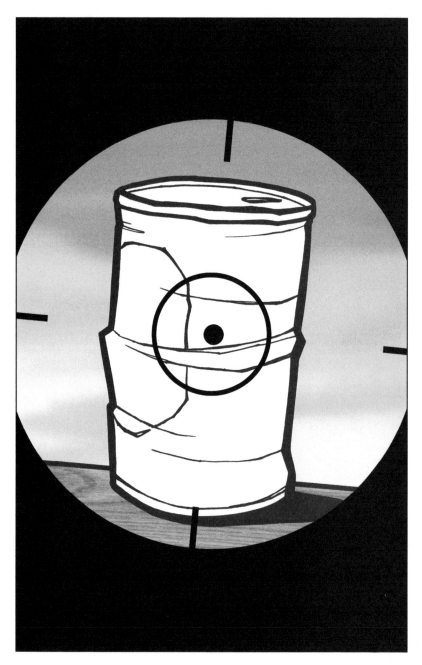

He shot carefully at his target, an old soup can. By now, his aim was nearly perfect.

After a few shots, Ethan paused to recheck his gun. He picked it back up again, held it straight, and aimed at another can.

The woods were completely silent. All that Ethan could hear was the movement of a few small creatures crunching through the leaves as they ran around on the ground.

Suddenly, Ethan saw a small squirrel scurrying around near his target. Ethan lowered his gun.

I wonder if I could hit that squirrel, he thought. He smiled. *I bet I could. I'm going to try it!*

Ethan raised the gun back up. He lowered his aim toward the ground. He looked at the squirrel through the gun's scope.

Slowly and carefully, Ethan pulled the trigger.

CHAPTER 7

Pfffft!

The gun fired. The shot was perfect.

The impact of the pellet made the squirrel fall over. Ethan took a deep breath. He couldn't believe it.

Ethan screamed happily. "Woo!" he yelled. He did a little dance. "Sweet!" he shouted to no one. "I did it! I hit a real target!"

Ethan knew that his father would be amazed at what he had done. He ran over and picked up the dead squirrel.

He carefully carried it out of the woods. Then he laid it down at the edge of his family's back yard.

He felt great. He wanted to see what else he could hit. For the rest of the afternoon, Ethan hunted squirrels and rabbits in the woods, all by himself.

After a couple of hours, he had collected five dead animals. There were three gray squirrels and two rabbits.

He gathered them up and brought them up closer to the house. He laid them down in the grass, side by side. He couldn't wait for his father to get home. His dad would be so proud.

He headed inside and watched some TV. Soon, he heard his father's car pull into the driveway.

Ethan ran out to the front porch. His father stepped out of the car and began walking toward the house.

"Dad, I have something awesome to show you," Ethan called. "It's in the back yard."

He led his dad around the house. They walked to the edge of the yard. Ethan pointed at the dead animals on the ground.

Ethan's father dropped his briefcase. He stared at Ethan. "What happened here?" he asked.

Ethan frowned. *Why isn't he excited?* he wondered. His father's face was not at all what he'd expected.

"I shot them all," Ethan said, still trying to be proud. "I got them all on the first shot, too. Well, almost all of them," he added.

"Aw, Ethan," his father said, shaking his head sadly. "You forgot the code." He crouched down near the dead animals and looked at them closely. He moved one of them with his shoe. There was no sign of life.

Suddenly, Ethan had a sick feeling in the pit of his stomach. The code. His dad was talking about the Hunter's Code. The promise that said he would never shoot an animal just for sport.

Finally, Ethan realized what he had done. He had killed five animals that he wasn't going to eat. He had broken the Hunter's Code.

"I'm sorry," Ethan said. "I forgot. I was just excited about being able to hit a moving target."

Dad shook his head and started walking away. He stopped and turned. He said, "Maybe you're not ready to be a hunter." Then he headed into the house.

CHAPTER 8
A REAL
HUNTING TRIP

Later that night, there was a knock on Ethan's bedroom door. Dad walked in. "I think I need to take your gun away for a while," he said. "I'm sorry, son, but you need to learn just how serious this is."

"I know it's serious," Ethan said.

"I don't think you do," his dad said. "Those were living animals. They didn't deserve to have their lives taken away for no reason."

Ethan's chin sank down to his chest. His eyes stared at the floor. He knew that his father was right. He also knew there was nothing he could say to make it any better.

* * *

For the next few days, Ethan tried not to think about hunting. All he could do was hope his father would give him another chance.

A few nights later, when Ethan's father came home from work, he had a surprise. He smiled at Ethan.

"Ethan, I'll pick you up from school tomorrow afternoon," he said. "You need to pack a bag tonight so that you're ready."

"Ready for what?" Ethan asked.

"Ready for a hunting trip," his father said.

Ethan's mouth dropped open. "Are you serious?" he asked, feeling shocked. "You're taking me hunting?"

Dad looked closely at Ethan. "I did not say I was taking you hunting," he said quietly. "I said I was taking you on a hunting trip."

"I don't get it," Ethan said. "What's the difference?"

"I'm taking you along. But you won't be hunting," his father explained. "We'll drive up tomorrow, and get to the cabin by tomorrow night. You'll come along with me on Saturday morning when I go out to hunt."

Ethan thought about it. He was excited to go on the trip, even if he didn't get to hunt.

"Okay," he said slowly. "That sounds pretty good, I guess."

"You need to see a real hunter hunt," Dad said. "Then you can see how a real hunter treats the game with respect. You can see how respectful a real hunter is to the land, too."

Ethan was disappointed that he wasn't going to be hunting. But he wanted his dad to trust him again with a gun. He had to really learn the Hunter's Code.

"It's not as good as really hunting," Ethan said. "But I know it's important. And I'm excited to go to the cabin."

"Great," Dad said. "Wait in the parking lot after school tomorrow. Get some sleep tonight." He left, shutting the door quietly behind him.

CHAPTER 9
THE CABIN

The next afternoon, Ethan waited in the school parking lot. Soon, his dad picked him up in the old pickup truck. They began the long drive up north to the cabin.

As the forest on the side of the road became thicker, Ethan got more excited. He couldn't wait to get to the cabin.

"Do you have any questions?" his dad asked. "About hunting, I mean."

Ethan thought for a minute. "I've always wondered how there are more deer every year," he said finally. "I mean, if the hunters shoot the deer, how come there are more the next year?"

Ethan's dad laughed. "Well, we don't shoot all the deer," he said. "And the Department of Natural Resources — the DNR — manages the hunt every year. They make sure that the hunters obey the rules about how many deer they shoot."

"What else does the DNR do for deer hunting?" Ethan asked.

"Well, they set other rules," Dad said. "There are also rules about shooting female deer and young deer. You can't shoot the young ones or the female deer unless you have a special paper. I only shoot bucks, the adult males."

As they got closer to the cabin, Ethan was so excited that he wasn't sure if he'd be able to sleep.

"You're sure we'll see some deer, right?" Ethan asked.

"Definitely," his father said. "This cabin is on land that lots of deer live on. We'll see deer."

The old pickup truck pulled into the dirt driveway that led to the cabin. It was dark out, but the truck's headlights lit up the cabin.

"We'll need to go to sleep right away," Ethan's father said as he parked the truck in front of the small wood cabin. "We'll be going out before first light."

CHAPTER 10
FIRST LIGHT

Ethan's father woke him up early the next morning. It was still dark outside.

They made a quick breakfast of eggs and bacon. Then they packed a cooler with snacks and bottles of water and got dressed for a day in the outdoors. They put on extra layers of clothes to stay warm.

When they headed out, it was dark. It was so cold that Ethan felt shocked.

As they walked the few hundred yards to his father's deer stand, Ethan warmed up. After all, he was wearing four layers of clothes.

The deer stand was a wood platform built in a tree. Ethan and his father climbed a ladder that led up to the platform. There were two folding chairs there.

They settled into the chairs. Ethan's father pulled out his gun and carefully placed it on his lap.

"Here," Ethan's father said. He reached into his backpack and pulled out a pair of binoculars. He handed them to Ethan. "Keep an eye out for me."

Ethan smiled. He hung the strap of the binoculars around his neck. "Okay, Dad," he said happily.

As the sun broke through on the horizon, it revealed a light mist that hung in the air all around them. Ethan glanced around the countryside.

His eye caught something big lying on the ground. He knew that he needed to keep quiet, so he didn't say anything to his dad. He just raised the binoculars up to his eyes.

The mist made it difficult to see what the brown shape on the ground was. "Dad," Ethan whispered. "What's that thing lying out there?"

"Where?" his father replied.

Ethan pointed to the spot. "Over there," he said.

His father grabbed the binoculars. He peered out at the lump in the distance.

"That's strange," Dad said. "Let's go check it out."

The pair climbed down from the deer stand. Then they walked slowly out toward the grassy area where they had spotted the strange brown lump.

As they walked, Ethan was glad that they were wearing bright orange hats. Other hunters would be able to see their movements. They wouldn't think Ethan and his dad were two deer walking along.

Suddenly, Ethan's father stopped. "Look here," he said. "There's a smear of blood on the bushes. But it's been raining a lot. The rain should have washed it away."

Soon, Ethan and his father reached the grassy area. Ethan slowly walked up to the brown lump.

It was a dead deer. The deer was lying on its side.

"I wonder who shot it," Ethan said quietly. He looked up at his father.

Ethan's father did not look happy. He leaned close to the deer to get a better look.

"You see the wounds, Ethan?" Dad asked. "Here, here, and here." He pointed to three different spots on the deer.

Ethan shook his head. "That's not what a real hunter does," he said. "Shooting the deer in that many places — that's not what you do if you plan to eat the meat. Whoever shot this deer just did it for the fun of shooting."

Ethan looked around for other clues. As the sun rose in the sky, it was beginning to burn away the mist.

Off in the distance, another 50 yards away, he saw another lump on the ground.

"Look, Dad," Ethan said. "What's that?"

Ethan and his dad walked over to the second lump. It was another dead deer. And like the first deer they'd found, it had been shot many times.

"I don't believe this," Ethan's father said.

"This one is small," Ethan said. "It isn't fully grown yet."

His father nodded. "It's less than a year old," he said. "Who could be doing this?"

CHAPTER 11
ALL THE WRONG REASONS

Suddenly, hunting didn't seem so important. Ethan felt the same pain his father was feeling.

Someone was out shooting deer and leaving them lying dead in the field. Whoever was hunting these deer was doing it for all the wrong reasons.

Ethan frowned. "Dad, I bet this didn't happen too long ago," he said.

"Why do you think that?" his father asked.

"If the deer had been here for a long time, wouldn't other animals have started to feed on them?" Ethan said.

"Good point, Ethan," his father said. "You're absolutely right."

"That means the people who shot these deer might still be around here somewhere," Ethan said. "We should try to track them and catch them."

Ethan's father frowned. "I don't think so. We don't know what kind of people we are dealing with here," he said. "It would be better for us to call the DNR. Then the DNR officers will take care of the problem."

"Okay," Ethan said. "I guess that makes sense."

"I'm sorry that this is going to cut into our hunting time," Ethan's father said.

"That's okay," Ethan told him. "Let's go call the DNR."

They used the cabin phone to call the DNR. Within an hour, two officers arrived. Dad told them what they'd found.

"Can you show us the dead deer?" one of the officers asked Ethan's dad.

"My son is the one who spotted the animals," Dad said. "Ethan, why don't you show these officers where you found the deer?"

It only took ten minutes for Ethan to lead the officers directly to the scene, where the first deer laid on the ground. He also showed the officers all the clues that he and his father had found.

When Ethan was done talking, one of the officers looked at Ethan's father and smiled. "You've got quite the young hunter here," the officer said. "He really knows his stuff. You must be awfully proud of him."

"I am," Ethan's father said. Ethan smiled from ear to ear.

Then Ethan's dad leaned over and whispered, "Let's get out of their way and head back to the cabin."

Ethan wanted to stay and watch the officers work, but he knew he'd be in the way. "Okay," he said.

A few hours later, there was a knock on the cabin door. It was the officers.

"Thanks to you, we found the men who were doing this," one officer said. "You were exactly right. They weren't far away."

"In fact, they were staying at a cabin just up the road," the other officer said. "They were just up here shooting animals for fun and leaving them on the ground. And they weren't done. They were going out to hunt again when we caught them today."

The first officer looked at Ethan and said, "Nice work, young man."

* * *

The next morning, Ethan and his father headed back to the deer stand. This time, as they walked along, Ethan noticed that his father was carrying a second gun.

When they got up in the stand, his father handed the second gun to Ethan.

"This is for me?" Ethan asked quietly, looking down at the gun.

"I've been keeping this for you," Dad said. "I was waiting for the day when you'd be ready to use a real gun. I think that day is today. Today, you proved that you would follow the Hunter's Code."

Ethan couldn't believe it. He took the gun in his hand and admired it. Then he stopped and thought about what it would mean to fire it.

He knew that whenever he pulled that trigger, it would only be for the right reasons. He would always follow the Hunter's Code.

— ABOUT THE AUTHOR —

Bob Temple lives in Rosemount, Minnesota, with his wife and three children. He has written more than thirty books for children. Over the years, he has coached more than twenty kids' soccer, basketball, and baseball teams. He also loves visiting classrooms to talk about his writing.

ABOUT THE ILLUSTRATOR

When Sean Tiffany was growing up, he lived on a small island off the coast of Maine. Every day, from sixth grade until he graduated from high school, he had to take a boat to get to school. When Sean isn't working on his art, he works on a multimedia project called "OilCan Drive," which combines music and art. He has a pet cactus named Jim.

— GLOSSARY —

antlers (ANT-lurz)—the large, branching, bony structures on the head of a deer. Antlers have more than one point.

binoculars (buh-NOK-yuh-lurz)—an instrument that you look through with both eyes to make distant things seem nearer

buck (BUHK)—a male deer

certificate (sur-TIF-uh-kit)—a piece of paper that officially states that something is a fact or has been completed

code (KODE)—a set of rules or agreements

firearm (FIRE-arm)—a weapon that shoots

pellet (PEL-it)—the small, hard ball that is shot out of an air gun

platform (PLAT-form)—a flat, raised surface

respect (ri-SPEKT)—treat with care

scope (SKOHP)—the part of the gun that is looked through to aim

trigger (TRIG-ur)—the lever on the gun that you pull to fire it

WHY DO PEOPLE HUNT?

Many people like to hunt because they enjoy the sport of it. Just like fishing, it can be fun to try to find an animal, such as a deer, and get it. But other people wonder how a person could shoot an animal as beautiful as a deer.

Humans have been hunting animals for thousands of years. Long before we had domesticated animals to eat, like cows, chickens, and turkeys, humans hunted wild animals in order to survive.

Nowadays, few humans need to hunt in order to survive. However, hunting still serves an important purpose. It helps keep the population of animals like deer at controllable levels. That allows the remaining animals to thrive and be healthy in their environments.

For example, Minnesota is one of the leading states for hunting white-tailed deer. In 2006 alone, more than 270,000 white-tailed deer were taken by hunters.

Think about how many deer there would be if hunting were not allowed to take place for even five years. That would mean more than a million more deer would be currently alive! There simply would not be enough food for all of those deer to live.

Many deer would starve, and sick animals would allow more disease to spread. By reducing the population of deer, the remaining deer are healthier.

Some people are against hunting, and some people aren't. It's up to each person to decide what they think.

— DISCUSSION — QUESTIONS

1. How did Ethan break the Hunter's Code?

2. In this book, Ethan learns that shooting an animal for fun is wrong. Some people think that shooting an animal for any reason is wrong. What do you think?

3. Why did Ethan's father bring him on the hunting trip?

— WRITING PROMPTS —

1. Pretend that you are Ethan. Write a postcard home to Ethan's mom from the hunting trip, telling her what happened.

2. Ethan wants to go hunting with his dad. Write about something you would like to do with a parent, teacher, or other adult.

3. At the end of this book, Ethan receives a real gun. Write about what you think happens next.

When his grandfather passes away, all that Daniel has left are stories of Big Larry, the monster fish Grandpa spent his life chasing. Can Daniel land the biggest catch of his life, or will he let Big Larry get away?

BY JAKE MADDOX

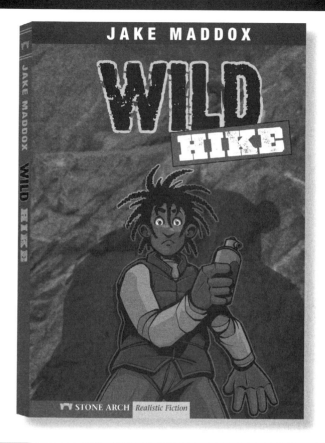

Nick has always loved camping, but his cousins don't listen to his warnings about campfires and bears, and they make fun of everything Nick does. When Devin finds himself in real danger, can Nick save him in time?

— INTERNET SITES —

Do you want to know more about subjects related to this book? Or are you interested in learning about other topics? Then check out FactHound, a fun, easy way to find Internet sites.

Our investigative staff has already sniffed out great sites for you!

Here's how to use FactHound:

1. Visit *www.facthound.com*

2. Select your grade level.

3. To learn more about subjects related to this book, type in the book's ISBN number: **9781434207821**.

4. Click the **Fetch It** button.

FactHound will fetch the best Internet sites for you!